AWAKE

To a New Life...

AWAKE

To a New Life...

And become the person
God created you to be!

A.D. Sikes

Published by Acknowledge LLC Publishing AT v5d

ISBN-13: 978-1-7340384-3-9

CONTENTS

INTRODUCTION

This story, about a guy named Jack, begins when he was at that fifty-something age. However, from God's perspective, his story relates to many people regardless of age, gender, and stage of life. Like many professed Christians, Jack assumed he was good with God and was ready with a convincing argument if needed. Fortunately, God leads him to discover the truth.

Jack had not been very religious or spiritual, but he always believed in God. And it was only because of his surroundings that any thought of God entered his mind. "There must be a God to have created something this beautiful," he said to himself. That happened early one Saturday morning, as he sat, alone with his coffee, on the dock of his lake home. He admired both the grandeur of the view along with the trophies that he worked hard to earn. He had a great house, three hundred feet of shoreline, and lake toys that kept him busy when he wasn't traveling on business. Jack wore the satisfaction of knowing he had already far surpassed his original life goals, and he was taking that moment to reflect. Then without intention, he said to God, "If there is any need for improvement, let me know." Although that statement could be viewed as an invitation, it was more of a boast. He knew he wasn't perfect, but he never considered God would see the need to respond to his invitation.

As a child, Jack attended church every Sunday. He knew about God from what he heard in church, but that was about it. Jack knew the Bible existed, and he believed it contained the truth about God, but he never wanted to go there. His limited knowledge of its contents came from references at Sunday church services. His parents taught him an underlying sense of right and wrong, and he tried to be good and be sorry when he wasn't. As an adult, he continued to attend church most Sundays, and he prayed when he found himself in a situation he couldn't control. Jack assumed he was good with God because he believed that Jesus was the Son of God who did what everyone know He did to save sinful man. Little did he know, God did not agree with Jack's assumptions.

As he began his adult life, Jack defined what essentially became his religion, even though he didn't think of it that way. It had two parts; one part pointed to God and the other to a song. The God-part had to do with scaling grades. When the entire class performed at less than expected grade levels in college, the professor often reduced the score needed to get a passing grade. So, he decided God would probably do the same since most people do not live the way God would expect. He thought when reasonably good people die and arrive at the pearly gates, God evaluates their performance relative to others, scales the grade, and admits most into Heaven. It made sense because Jack believed God loves His creations and wants them to be with Him in Heaven.

The song-part of Jack's religion came at the impressionable age of twenty when he heard Frank Sinatra sing *My Way.* It was a powerful performance by a man who was a proven success. He studied the lyrics and decided my-way would be his approach to life. As the song says, Jack knew that my-way would lead to a few regrets, but in the end, regrets wouldn't matter. At his invincible age, he knew he might bite off more than he could chew, but he dismissed the pain of losing and decided his my-way life would be amusing. He might occasionally face doubt, but he would stand tall and push it out.

Depending on himself, Jack would be free to say and do whatever he felt. However, he would also try to keep God in mind because he wanted to present a convincing case that he was a reasonably good person with good intentions. The two components of Jack's approach seemed to fit together for a young guy about to turn twenty-one. Then based on his accomplishments of the next thirty years, he confirmed his approach to life must be right.

This story begins not long after that when Jack tosses out that boastful invitation to God to let him know if there is any real need for improvement. Jack got much more than he expected.

NIGHT 1

I doubt it, God, but let me know if there is any real need for improvement.

It was a little unusual that Jack had the entire week to work from home. He routinely traveled for his consulting job and was typically home only on weekends. He planned to prepare for the upcoming week and complete a few home projects.

For the first half of his career, he had a real job, but now had flexibility in how he used his time and talents. Educated as an engineer, Jack advanced to middle-management positions before starting his second career as a management consultant. In that role, his clients reaped measurable benefits by following his advice. With an excellent track record, life was good for Jack and his family, so he could not help but conclude his approach to life was right.

He planned to get most of his work done in the first couple of days and enjoy the remainder of the week at home. Jack loved working above the garage in his home office – a great hideaway with views of the lake, space to walk around, and privacy to think, work and even talk to himself. He had a coffee maker, microwave, small refrigerator, and bathroom, so he was set for the day.

Later that day, after a casual dinner with his wife, they watched the news and did a few things before their evening television time. He checked his email, including a few internet searches for items he wanted to buy, and then settled in to catch up on recorded shows that accumulate when he was out of town. Then, off to bed where they both enjoyed reading as a way to clear their minds for a restful sleep. Jack's typical evening became the most unusual night.

The Dream

> The setting of his dream was a combination of all of the most beautiful scenes Jack had observed during his lifetime, when he would stop and say something like, "There must be a God to have created this beauty." And somehow, even before hearing Him speak, Jack knew that God would be part of this dream. Surprisingly, he was not afraid of what was happening as this dream unfolded, nor was he overly excited. It was like one of those peaceful times on the dock when he absorbed the beauty of the world around him.
>
> Then he heard God's presence, say: "Yes, Jack, you do require improvement. Your assumptions about God and life are not right, and you need to know the truth." There was a short pause allowing Jack to take it in. God then concluded the dream by inviting him to ask one question each day that God would answer in a dream. He added that it would be Jack's choice to go forward with these dreams, and the vision was gone.

Jack slept soundly throughout the night and awoke refreshed, but the strange dream was the first thing on his mind. He brushed it off, got ready, ate breakfast, and went to his office to work. But thoughts of the dream continued to surface throughout the day. The idea that God would be talking to him was unlikely because his life was going so well. "After all," he muttered, "Why would God be talking to me?" He figured the dream had to be a subconscious connection to a movie or TV show he had seen. Maybe it was from something he ate – he did have chili for dinner that night.

Reflect and Discuss

So, what do you think? If you were sure He would reply, would you be bold enough to ask God if there is a need for you to improve? Are you possibly assuming things about God and about life that may not be true?

NIGHT 2

If this dream thing is real, why me?

It wasn't typical for something to bother Jack, but last night's dream did. Rather than continue to think about it, he decided to resolve the issue once and for all. He would ask God one question and then be able to forget the whole thing because he knew the dream would not return. As he climbed into bed, Jack mentally tossed out this question in case God was listening: "If this dream thing is real, why me?" Then, after turning to the novel he had been reading, he was sound asleep within ten minutes.

The Dream

> The setting and sense of this dream were the same as the previous night, and he heard the same comforting voice say, "Jack, I am giving you this opportunity because you asked for it. Also, I know that you are finally interested in knowing what it would be like to live God's way rather than Frank's my-way."

Jack slept soundly, but as morning broke, he was suddenly wide-awake thinking about the dream. It was so brief that he wondered if he had imagined it. He reasoned most dreams seem to go on and on, but this one was over in a moment. He was close to convincing himself of that when he remembered the reference to 'Frank's my-way.' That was too close to home to dismiss. Jack hadn't heard the song or thought about it recently, but the my-way of living was still part of his strategy. God also said he had asked for an opportunity to hear from God, but he could not recall. It was a rough start to a day where he had more than enough to do.

Reflect and Discuss

Do you think this was the first time in Jack's life that God tried to communicate with him? Has God tried to communicate with you through other people or through situations that you've faced? Think back and try to remember times in your life when you dismissed what God was telling you because you were determined to do things your way.

NIGHT 3

So, what is the problem?

Still in disbelief these dreams were happening, Jack couldn't stop thinking God described this as an opportunity. He argued an 'opportunity' is optional, while a 'need' is mandatory. At the same time, Jack reasoned maybe he had a real need to get right with God, and he would see the opportunity if he did. Either way, the fact that God was talking to him about changing his my-way approach to life must have something to do with a problem.

Jack had no idea what problem God was seeing. He tried to be good and did most things other Christians did as far as he knew. His life was great, indicating he was doing something right – a good family, decent values, successful career, and material rewards to show his approach to life was working. "So, what is the problem?" That was the next question, but he thought God must have more significant issues to deal with than him.

Jack was usually good at assessing situations and people, but this dream thing had him feeling baffled, confused, and defensive. Nevertheless, he decided to continue because God gave him the option to stop the dream dialogue at any time. However, falling to sleep wasn't easy that night because he was inviting God to identify a problem he did not want to know he had.

The Dream

The dream looked the same, but Jack was not at peace as he waited for the presence of God to appear. That was the situation for an extended time, causing him to think back on his life. He also thought about the assumptions that were the foundation of his life strategy. The first was God would be scaling the grades for people to get into Heaven. He told himself it made sense, but he wondered if it was true. At the same time, he questioned how God deals with the fact nobody is good enough to get into Heaven. Even if people are forgiven for doing evil things, Jack reasoned they would continue to do wrong when in Heaven because people are who they are. If that happened, then Heaven wouldn't be very heavenly. Furthermore, if God changes people to be permanently good after they die, why doesn't He do that here on earth? In the dream, Jack couldn't figure out what God was thinking, but he acknowledged he never tried to do that when he was awake.

Suddenly, something was appearing across the sky that snapped Jack out of the discussion with himself. *Therefore, if anyone is in Christ, he is a new creation; the old has gone, the new has come!* (2 Corinthians 5:17). The presence of God was suddenly everywhere. He explained how this verse from the Bible describes Jack's problem: "You are not the new creation in Christ that you are called to be. Instead, you are the same person who was born some five decades earlier; and who has never received my Son, Jesus, as both Savior and Lord. Jack, you can be the person I call you to be, but that will never happen by taking your my-way approach to life." God went on to say this earthly life is the time to become a new creation in Christ and grow toward the perfection of God's family in Heaven.

The next topic was Jack's assumptions. "Your assumption of being good enough is entirely wrong. No person is good enough to live in God's presence, and you can do nothing to make yourself good. As recorded in Luke 18:19, Jesus said, *No one is good – except God alone.*

Another issue is your assumption that God must have more significant issues to deal with than you. Again, as Jesus said in Matthew 18:12-14: *What do you think? If a man owns a hundred sheep, and one of them wanders away, will he not leave the ninety-nine on the hills and go to look for the one that wandered off? And if he finds it, truly I tell you, he is happier about that one sheep than about the ninety-nine that did not wander off. In the same way your Father in heaven is not willing that any of these little ones should perish.*"

As he awoke, there was no doubt God was communicating with him, and it was clear God saw him as a 'lost sheep' who was in danger of perishing. Jack realized his thinking and assumptions were not aligned with God, but he had no idea why.

At the same time, God seemed to be offering the solution of making him into a *new creation in Christ* – which he certainly did not understand. In only a few days, Jack went from having everything under control to learning he was not good with God, he was wandering like a lost sheep, and he needed to be made into a new person. He was typically able to handle unexpected situations pretty well, but not this. At the same time, Jack was amazed God was personally interested in him.

Reflect and Discuss

Perhaps you understand why God would answer Jack with the Word of God in 2 Corinthians 5:17. Put yourself in the position of someone who has never seen that verse or does not know what it means. What other questions would you (or do you) have to understand what God is saying?

NIGHT 4

Why haven't I heard about this 'new creation' idea, and what does it mean?

Throughout the day, Jack's thoughts were as scrambled as the eggs he had for breakfast. Why didn't he know about the need to be a new creation after years of attending Sunday church services? He had heard Jesus' parable of the lost sheep, but never considered himself one of them. At the same time, it was easier to accept being a lost sheep than a new creation. "What would that do to who I am and everything I am trying to accomplish? What would people think of me if I somehow became someone else? If other Christians have become new creations, why do I not know who is and who is not?"

He considered going to the Bible to see more about that 2 Corinthians verse, but the Bible always seemed so difficult to understand. Besides, he wondered why God does not merely forgive people and allow them to start over. Why should he have to become new? Hardened criminals maybe, but not people like him. It didn't make sense, but he was still curious to continue this exceptional communication with God. He realized he had a lot to learn and felt better after realizing God saw him as being lost rather than bad or evil. At the same time, it was clear that only God is good.

Jack had a mind full of questions but tried to honor God's direction to limit each dream to one. Plus, he was getting more than he could handle with one question. Nevertheless, his question for that night had two parts. "Why haven't I heard about this 'new creation' idea, and what does it mean?

The Dream

The presence of God said, "First of all, your need to become a new creation is not an idea - it is a reality that the Son of God suffered, died, and rose from the dead to provide." His words were kind but firm, and Jack received the message.

God said the 2 Corinthians 5:17 verse had been presented to him in church on more than one occasion, but he never made an effort to relate it to himself. "You are one of many people Jesus describes in Matthew 13:13. *Though seeing, they do not see; though hearing, they do not hear or understand.*"

He continued saying Jack's my-way approach gives him a calloused heart that prevents him from understanding God's Word. "However, when a person truly receives Jesus as Savior and Lord, he is given a new heart as promised in Ezekiel 36:26-27. *I will give you a new heart and put a new spirit in you; I will remove from you your heart of stone and give you a heart of flesh. And I will put my Spirit in you and move you to follow my decrees and be careful to keep my laws.*"

With that background, God addressed Jack's question. "The need to be a 'new creation in Christ' is certainly not new. It originated when Adam and Eve first sinned in the Garden of Eden. Because their perfect righteousness was destroyed, it was no longer possible for them to live in God's presence. Furthermore, they could not recreate their righteousness."

> As this dream concluded, God told Jack to go to the Bible and read about Jesus' conversation with Nicodemus.

He finished the night and woke up feeling disappointed his my-way approach kept him from understanding God's Word. He thought about all of those years of attending Sunday church services and learning very little. At the same time, he had to admit he never wanted to know much about God, so he could see why God said his heart was hardened.

Reflect and Discuss

Even if you believe in God, where are you on the scale of needing Him? On the low end (zero), you have no interest in anything related to God. The high end (ten) means you desperately need Him, even if your life is good.

Do you know what God means about being made into a new creation? Why did God not simply forgive Adam and Eve and allow them to start over?

NIGHT 5

Why not just forgive people and give them a new start?

A busy day was planned to prepare for the next week of business travel, and now he had an assignment from God to read about Nicodemus and Jesus discussing the need to be reborn. He decided to get his work out of the way, then concentrate on his dream assignment. Of course, the work-related activities didn't quite go as planned, and several issues came up throughout the day. It was nearly dinner time when he finally turned to Nicodemus. Having no idea where in the Bible to find that story, Jack did an on-line search to find it in the third chapter of the Gospel of John. He read the first twenty-one verses but didn't understand what Jesus was telling Nicodemus. However, he didn't feel too bad because Nicodemus also did not understand, and he was a scholar and teacher of Scripture. Jack then stopped for dinner and his evening routine.

As he prepared to go to bed, Jack struggled to find the right question for that night because the Nicodemus story seemed too confusing. He did think of a simple question and decided to go with it. "Why not just forgive people and give them a new start? Why do they have to be reborn as a new creation?"

The Dream

The dream developed again, and Jack was at peace with what

was taking place. He knew he did not understand everything God was telling him, but he continued to be curious and amazed that God was working with him.

The presence of God told Jack that his question was logical from a human perspective, but there is so much about God that human logic cannot imagine. He spoke a verse from Isaiah 55:8 NLT: *"My thoughts are nothing like your thoughts," says the LORD. "And my ways are far beyond anything you could imagine."* From that, Jack understood why he was totally lost. His hardened heart was keeping him from comprehending the Word of God, and God's thoughts and ways were beyond his imagination.

However, God continued to guide him toward understanding why more than forgiveness is needed to restore man to righteousness. "A person must sincerely ask for God's forgiveness and believe and receive Jesus as Savior and Lord. At the same time, justice must be served, and the wages of sin must be paid. Justice is a foundation of God. *Righteousness and justice are the foundation of your throne; love and faithfulness go before you* (Psalm 89:14). And from Romans 6:23: *For the wages of sin is death, but the gift of God is eternal life in Christ Jesus, our Lord.* In other words, the price to restore man to the righteousness needed to live in God's presence could only be paid by God Himself. In that way, the Son of God had to suffer, die, and rise from the dead to restore man to have the righteousness needed for eternal life with God."

He began the day feeling good because he understood the big picture of God's answer. He noted the verse numbers and found time to reread them and make notes about the dream. He was beginning to understand why forgiveness alone would not provide the righteousness needed to live with God for eternity. He always believed the Son of God died for our sins, but he now saw why the wages of sin are so high.

Jack likened the damage caused by sin to what he knew about DNA. In today's terminology, it was like Adam and Eve's perfect DNA was changed when they sinned, and that sinful DNA was inherited by every person born after them. They could not modify their DNA back to its original state. Only God could change a sinner's DNA back to righteousness, but at an extremely high cost. His DNA analogy wasn't in the Bible and wasn't exactly what happened, but it allowed him to remember why Jesus was the only way for sinners to be made righteous again.

Reflect and Discuss

Discuss why God's forgiveness alone does not allow people to start over with a clean slate. Think about the fact that God requires justice to be served and the wages of sin to be paid.

We think of the horrors of Jesus' suffering to pay the wages of our sins, but also imagine how the Father suffered at the same time. Now think of how He must feel when most people in this world continue to reject Him and His invitation to become a new creation in Christ.

NIGHT 6

Do other Christians know about all of this?

Jack and his first cup of coffee were back on the dock early on Saturday morning. He was amazed these dream communications with God resulted from a comment he made some time ago from that very spot. As he looked at the peaceful beauty around him, Jack was beginning to appreciate the opportunity to know about God and His plan for life. At the same time, he feared how his life might change if he allowed himself to get too close to God. However, it was the weekend, and Jack decided to go forward with his plans to have fun and relax. He was confident a question would come to mind before bedtime.

It turned out to be a carefree day of fun, and as he settled into bed for the night, he asked God if most other Christians know what he was learning.

The Dream

> The setting was the same, but somehow the intensity of everything was higher. The scene was more vivid, as were the subtle sounds in the background. Jack thought he had asked a simple question, but this preview indicated more than a casual answer.
>
> God told Jack that the following words of Jesus need to be heard by many professed Christians who are falsely assuming their saving relationship with Jesus. *"Not*

everyone who says to me, 'Lord, Lord,' will enter the kingdom of heaven, but the one who does the will of my Father who is in heaven. On that day many will say to me, 'Lord, Lord, did we not prophesy in your name, and cast out demons in your name, and do many mighty works in your name?' And then will I declare to them, 'I never knew you; depart from me, you workers of lawlessness.'" (Matthew 7:21-23 ESV).

Knowing Jack could not process His message, the Father continued with this explanation. "As part of the Sermon on the Mount, Jesus spoke to people who were professing to be his followers. His words describe what will happen on judgment day when *many* professed Christians will be turned away from entering Heaven. They will plead their case on the works they claimed to do in Jesus' name. But He will dismiss them saying, *I never knew you; depart from me...*" A pause allowed Jack to replay the message of that verse before God explained that Jesus does not recognize many people as true believers. Those people may accept Him as the Son of God and Savior, but they have not received Him and do not have a heartfelt faith in Him as both Savior and Lord. As such, they have not been reborn as new creations and not adopted as children of God."

When that happens to you Jack, Jesus will greet you on that day with open arms, as He describes in Matthew 25-23. *Well done, good and faithful servant! You have been faithful with a few things; I will put you in charge of many things. Come and share your master's happiness.*"

Jack woke up on Sunday morning feeling convicted. He could not ignore the fact God said he was not yet a new creation in Christ. That was clear. At the same time, he felt the love and kindness with which God delivered the message; and he sensed God was inviting him to know Jesus and be known by him. So, he had hope.

Reflect and Discuss

Were you aware of Jesus' prophesy in Matthew 7:21-23? Do you understand why Jesus will be dismissing those multitudes of people who profess to be Christians? Can you think of any excuse He will accept? Is Jesus' message of this verse periodically delivered at your church?

NIGHT 7

This is a lot for me to process, and I am interested. But, can I have some time?

He began Sunday morning, thinking the past week was like none other. Preparing to go to Sunday church service, Jack wondered if something unusual would happen there. No telling what that might be, but he never imagined having nightly dreams with God. His wife sensed Jack's preoccupation and gave him some space.

The service was typical, and Jack spent the afternoon more or less in a zone as he grilled the lunch meal, took a short nap, and packed for his trip to the airport early the next morning. He had many other questions but didn't want to add to the overload that continued to spin around in his mind. So, he decided to ask God for some time before continuing his dreams. He would use the time to review the dreams, research some of the verses, and envision what might happen if he continues down this path.

The Dream

The splendid setting of the dream was again in place as the presence of God lovingly told him to use the time wisely. Then this Bible verse appeared in the sky much like the introduction to a Star Wars movie:

There is a time for everything, and a season for every activity under the heavens:

a time to be born and a time to die,
a time to plant and a time to uproot,
a time to kill and a time to heal,
a time to tear down and a time to build,
a time to weep and a time to laugh,
a time to mourn and a time to dance,
a time to scatter stones and a time to gather them,
a time to embrace and a time to refrain from embracing,
a time to search and a time to give up,
a time to keep and a time to throw away,
a time to tear and a time to mend,
a time to be silent and a time to speak,
a time to love and a time to hate,
a time for war and a time for peace (Ecclesiastes 3:1-8).

It was a short dream for a short night as he woke up early for his two-hour drive to the airport. He felt relieved to have some time and space to figure out what to do next in light of his work demands of the next several weeks.

Reflect and Discuss

Since Jack is facing a decision regarding his eternal salvation, are you surprised God would give Jack whatever time he wanted? Are you surprised Jack would ask for time and space, considering he is not assured of his eternal salvation? Isn't it easy to defer that decision, especially if not being confronted by God?

DREAM BREAK

Jack planned to spend the evenings of his business travel week to focus exclusively on the dreams and the verses from them; in fact, he looked forward to doing that. However, Monday was more demanding than expected, and he had to go to dinner with the client to continue discussions. That went well, but by the time he got back to the hotel, he was spent.

Then off to another client for a couple of days, which also took extra time and attention. Finally, by Thursday evening, Jack started on his other priority. It was a slow start because he had been so engaged with his consulting activities. It was almost like, "What dreams, and why am I even thinking about God?"

For the next three weeks, the demands of Jack's work and his weekend activities at home took most of his time and attention. Nevertheless, he didn't give up and eventually got through his review of the dreams and more.

Jack's Analysis

Jack concluded that his my-way approach to life was contrary to God's way, but he didn't know much about God's way other than keeping the ten commandments. Jack thought he had been aligned with most of them, but admitted not knowing all ten. Having no idea where in the Bible to find them, he discovered a BibleGateway website showing them in Exodus 20. He was doing okay on most of the commandments, but a few might be more comprehensive than he thought. For example, he had not been thinking of his other priorities and interests as false gods, but maybe God does. Nevertheless, Jack did not believe his infractions would be worthy of God's attention.

The next topic was that of being a new creation in Christ. After rereading John 3:1-15, he was still more confused than Nicodemus. He also noticed that the "Spirit" was somehow part of being reborn as a new creation in Christ. Then he saw John 3:16 saying: *For God so loved the world that he gave his one and only Son, that whoever believes in him shall not perish but have eternal life.* Jack decided all of those elements must be pieces of the puzzle of becoming a new creation, but he could not see how they fit together. The John 3:16 part seemed easy to understand but he concluded God must have a different definition of what it means to believe.

The last dream topic he thought about was the Matthew 7:21-23 verse, and that had his attention. As an assumed Christian, Jack based his Christianity on John 3:16, *that whoever believes in him shall not perish but have eternal life.* It was easy to believe the major events of Jesus' life and then go on living his my-way life. Now in Matthew 7:21-23, he sees God's definition of 'believe' must be more extensive than his.

Frustration was Jack's first reaction, thinking God was making this confusing. But then he cooled down when he remembered from one of the dreams God referenced a verse from Isaiah saying, *"My thoughts are nothing like your thoughts and my ways are far beyond anything you can imagine."* So, Jack again read Matthew 7:21-23, trying to see why Jesus will be turning away many people who think they believe. These words of Jesus got his attention: *"I never knew you."* Jack admitted he knew a few things about Jesus from attending church, but he couldn't come close to saying he knew more than highlights of Jesus' life.

Making It Happen

Being encouraged with his analysis, Jack wanted to begin a relationship with Jesus. As proof of his intentions, he would start his relationship with Jesus before getting back to the Father with more dream questions. He was good at developing business and social relationships, so he knew what he would do.

He decided to start each day in prayer and then turn to Jesus throughout the day, as needed, to make decisions that would please God. Also, from his business background, he knew it would be useful to review his performance at the end of each day. He had good intentions, but could not see he was using his my-way approach to establish a relationship with Jesus.

Jack did that for the next three weeks with mixed feelings on how well it was working. He was pretty good at starting and ending each day by turning to God in prayer, but prayer in the morning was usually on the run, and it was a passing thought at night as he drifted off to sleep. He often forgot to turn to Jesus in situations that came at him throughout the day. Plus, there wasn't time to have a discussion with Jesus in the middle of real-life situations. Nevertheless, he made a sincere attempt and decided it was time to continue with questions and dreams.

Reflect and Discuss

Is Jack on the right track? How do you think God will respond?

NIGHT 8

I'm back and trying to make it happen. What's next?

Seven weeks had passed since his last dream event, and Jack was excited to see how God viewed his efforts and hopefully learn more about what to do next. He was trying to relate to Jesus, pray more often, and even read the Bible a little. So, as he prepared for bed, Jack asked God to visit once again in a dream.

Suddenly, it was morning, and he was surprised and confused; there had been no dream. He was also disappointed because he thought God would be congratulating him on his efforts. This dream void continued for several days, and Jack was concerned God had written him off like those assumed Christians at the final judgment. He didn't know what to do except pray, and he did. Finally, on Saturday night of that week, Jack was again visited by God in a dream.

The Dream

> The sense of this dream was different, but every bit as spectacular as before. Jack was excited but also anxious as he awaited the presence of God. At one point, Jack thought the entire night would go on that way as he reviewed his recent efforts to relate to Jesus.
>
> Finally, this verse appeared: *Humble yourselves, therefore, under God's mighty hand, that he may lift you up in due time* (1 Peter 5:6). There was a long pause as Jack felt God

watching his every breath and hearing his every thought. He was confused by what was taking place as well as by the verse God proclaimed. He was expecting a big attaboy, but nothing happened. Several life situations flashed through his mind to emphasize that 'humble' was not his style, and 'time' was something he tried too hard to manage.

God then told Jack that verse was for him and for many other people who insist on doing things their way. "*Humble yourselves* means surrendering who you are to be the person Jesus is calling you to be. *Time* is another point of that verse you need to consider as explained in 2 Peter 3:8: *But do not forget this one thing, dear friends: With the Lord, a day is like a thousand years, and a thousand years are like a day.*"

"Jack, during your dream break you struggled with what it means to believe in Jesus. Referring to John 3:16, you concluded that you have always believed in Jesus as the Son of God who died to pay the price of sin and rose back to new life. But you could not understand how Jesus will be dismissing people as He said in Matthew 7:21-23, because you decided those people also believed in Jesus and did good works in His name. You were right in concluding that God must have a different definition of what it means to believe.

"At this point, your belief is merely accepting the fact that Jesus is the Son of God and Savior. But that is not enough, even if you think you are doing good works in His name. My Word in John 1:12-13 reads: *Yet to all who did receive him, to those who believed in his name, he gave the right to become children of God— children born not of natural descent, nor of human decision or a husband's will, but born of God.* You see that My definition of belief in the one true

God includes your commitment to receive Jesus as both Savior and Lord of your life going forward. Another way to see that is in terms of trust as shown in Proverbs 3:5-6. *Trust in the LORD with all your heart and lean not on your own understanding; in all your ways submit to him, and he will make your paths straight.*

"Believing and receiving Jesus is your all-in commitment to submit to Him in everything you think, say and do. You need help from God to pull it off, but the commitment is yours to make. Also know that your commitment to believe must be absolute, knowing you will face hardships along the way and opposition from the enemy. Jesus taught this in this parable in Luke 4:3-8. *'Listen! A farmer went out to sow his seed. As he was scattering the seed, some fell along the path, and the birds came and ate it up. Some fell on rocky places, where it did not have much soil. It sprang up quickly, because the soil was shallow. But when the sun came up, the plants were scorched, and they withered because they had no root. Other seed fell among thorns, which grew up and choked the plants, so that they did not bear grain. Still other seed fell on good soil. It came up, grew and produced a crop, some multiplying thirty, some sixty, some a hundred times.'* Jesus then explained this parable by saying: '*The farmer sows the word. Some people are like seed along the path, where the word is sown. As soon as they hear it, Satan comes and takes away the word that was sown in them. Others, like seed sown on rocky places, hear the word and at once receive it with joy. But since they have no root, they last only a short time. When trouble or persecution comes because of the word, they quickly fall away. Still others, like seed sown*

> *among thorns, hear the word; but the worries of this life, the deceitfulness of wealth and the desires for other things come in and choke the word, making it unfruitful. Others, like seed sown on good soil, hear the word, accept it, and produce a crop—some thirty, some sixty, some a hundred times what was sown'* (Luke 4:14-20).
>
> "Jack, your all-in commitment to trust in the Lord is the seed on the good soil of belief and faith that welcomes Jesus to know you. We will later discuss what happens as you receive that Gift and become a new creation in Christ. In the meantime, remember what I said at the start of this dream, *humble yourself under God's mighty hand, that he may lift you up in due time*."

The long dream ended, but a fitful night continued. As he prepared for the day, Jack buried his head in his hands from expecting God to praise him for his efforts. At the same time, he was happy to learn how God described what it means to believe. Jack knew that his trust had always been in himself rather than God, but he still could not imagine how that could work in the real world of daily life. Hopefully, God would be willing to answer more of his questions.

Reflect and Discuss

Reflect on 1 Peter 5:6 regarding being humble in God's presence. How should that translate to daily life? Also, consider what it means to truly believe and receive Jesus as Savior and Lord of your life going forward. Do you see how Jesus' parable of the good soil relates?

NIGHT 9

Is it wrong to want to know more before submitting to follow Christ?

Working from his home office was what he needed that day. God's reply made enough of an impact that Jack put his consulting work aside and focused on his ongoing discussion with God. Realizing something good must be happening, he was still discouraged. Nevertheless, he tried to clear his mind and began with prayer. He didn't recite a common prayer and didn't try to be formal. He paced the floor and spoke out loud about everything on his mind, sometimes repeating himself because of his confusion. Then he began writing to God to bring out some of his buried thoughts. Later, he would continue that practice as a prayer journal, but now he was trying to understand his thoughts and feelings as he communicated with God. He had no idea how long that went on, but he knew he was humbling himself to God, and it wasn't easy.

His thoughts then turned to doubt that God's way would be practically possible. How could he handle his demanding job, family life, and personal interests by being humble and not pressing to make things happen? Another question was the urgency of becoming a new creation in Christ. He was still concerned about how his life would change and wondered if it was wrong to hold back and ask a few more questions. That would be his next question.

Feeling hungry, Jack realized that he had been communicating with

God for over three hours! He felt better, even without knowing God's answer to his prayer. Clearing all of that from his mind, he ate lunch then had a great afternoon with his wife and friends at the lake.

The Dream

Although he was sound asleep, Jack was excited to see his dream was happening. The presence of God made his heart smile with joy even before hearing God's message of encouragement. God told him people take many paths to find Jesus as Savior and Lord. Some people wait to face a traumatic situation until they fully surrender to Christ without knowing and caring about how their life will change. Others want a preview of a new life in Christ. He referenced *The Case for Christ* book by Lee Strobel as an example of a man of his generation who diligently searched for answers before finally submitting in faith to believe and receive Jesus.

God then turned to the subject of prayer. "Jack, that three-hour period in your home office the previous morning was real prayer communication with Me. You did humble yourself and became honest with yourself. It was a good start and you will learn from the Bible there are many ways to effectively pray to Me. Here are a few examples."

Prayers of Worship *Worship the Father in the Spirit and in truth* (John 4:23-24). *Sing to the Lord, all the earth; proclaim his salvation day after day. Declare his glory among the nations, his marvelous deeds among all peoples. For great is the Lord and most worthy of praise; he is to be* *feared above all gods. For all the gods of the nations are idols, but the Lord made the heavens. Splendor and majesty are before him: strength and joy are in his dwelling place* (1 Chronicles 16:23-27).

Prayers of Thanksgiving *And whatever you do, whether in word or deed, do it all in the name of the Lord Jesus, giving thanks to God the Father through him* (Colossians 3:17).

Prayers of Spiritual Warfare Ephesians 6:10-12 says, *Finally, be strong in the Lord and in his mighty power. Put on the full armor of God, so that you can take your stand against the devil's schemes. For our struggle is not against flesh and blood, but against the rulers, against the authorities, against the powers of this dark world and against the spiritual forces of evil in the heavenly realms.*

Prayers of Intercession *I urge, then, first of all, that petitions, prayers, intercession and thanksgiving be made for all people* (1 Timothy 2:1).

Prayers of Request *Do not be anxious about anything, but in every situation, by prayer and petition, with thanksgiving, present your requests to God* (Philippians 4:6).

In summary, the presence of God told Jack that his questions and God's answers will continue well beyond the moment he becomes a new creation in Christ. He encouraged Jack to continue with his questions, but to remember his decision to believe and receive Jesus is ultimately a matter of faith.

After feeling hopeless the previous morning, Jack was again encouraged. He would continue with his questions and pray to be humble and patient with God. Jack believed, at some point, he would go all-in to believe and receive Jesus, but in the meantime, he would enjoy this quest to learn more about God and His plan for life.

Reflect and Discuss

Jack three-hour prayer is a step at being honest with himself about his relationship with God. He is concerned about risking the control he thinks he has and the life he has been enjoying. Is it possible to keep control and also believe and receive Jesus as Savior? Reflect on the verses describing other types of prayer communication that we need to have with God.

NIGHT 10

Why is this life the way it is, and is there any hope?

Yesterday he experienced fervent prayer, so today he got up a little early to do it again – albeit for a much shorter duration. Although he had more questions about topics already covered, Jack felt free to put them on hold and ask about life in general. He couldn't imagine God intended the chaos, hurt, hardship, crime, and evil that everyone has to endure. So why is this life the way it is, and is there any hope?

The Dream

Although Jack could not see the image of God, His presence was everywhere. He previously heard the term 'omnipresent' and was now experiencing God's omnipresence in both sight and sound.

God began by saying this dream summary would not come close to describing the innumerable and repetitive ways generations of people continue to destroy His once perfect creation. People had the responsibility to manage the earth, along with all of the resources needed to do that without chaos, death, damage, and destruction.

The ability of people to choose is part of God's providential plan for this earthly life. There was a brief pause as Jack thought about some of the big decisions he made throughout his life, and he wondered if they aligned with God's plan. God answered his thought, saying his choices are eternally significant, and he is responsible for them. He then proclaimed these words from 2 Corinthians 5:10: *"For we must all appear before the judgment seat of Christ, so that each of us may receive what is due us for the things done while in the body, whether good or bad.*

"This earthly life contains the chaos, hurt, hardship, crime, and evil because most people choose the lies and deceptions of the devil rather than the truth of God. People turn away from God and invite evil into their lives, just as the first people did." Referring again to the Bible, God described how Adam and Eve challenged God's sovereignty in favor of inviting evil into their lives.

"Their nourishment originally came from the Tree of Life as described in the Book of Genesis. It was clear they must not eat from the Tree of the Knowledge of Good and Evil. *Now the LORD God had planted a garden in the east, in Eden; and there he put the man he had formed. The LORD God made all kinds of trees grow out of the ground—trees that were pleasing to the eye and good for food. In the middle of the garden were the tree of life and the tree of the knowledge of good and evil. And the LORD God commanded the man, You are free to eat from any tree in the garden; but you must not eat from the tree of the knowledge of good and evil, for when you eat from it, you will certainly die* (Genesis 2:8-9,16-17).

"The choice for all people today is the same – choose Christ Jesus and the Tree of Life or choose Satan and the Tree of the Knowledge of Good and Evil. Because most of the billions of people want to experience both evil and good, the results are chaos, destruction, and death."

"And yes, Jack, there is both hope and assurance of the perfect life as I created it to be. Jesus told you to pray for My kingdom to come on earth as it is in Heaven. Believing and receiving Jesus assures you of that life in Heaven for eternity. In the meantime, there is hope as I say in 2 Chronicles 7:14: *If my people, who are called by my name, will humble themselves and pray and seek my face and turn from their wicked ways, then I will hear from heaven, and I will forgive their sin and will heal their land.*"

As he awoke, Jack laid still thinking about the hope, assurance, and peace God was offering. Although God said there was hope, he couldn't imagine what it would take for billions of people to humble themselves, pray, seek to know God, and turn from their wicked ways. But Jack believed there was room for him to do that and experience some of God's kingdom in his life on earth.

Reflect and Discuss

Did you know about the two trees that God describes in Genesis? Why would God create this perfect world along with a test that would result in its destruction?

What would it take to get the attention of many people throughout this earth to humble themselves, pray, seek the face of God, and turn from their wicked ways?

NIGHT 11

Why does Your plan allow Satan to destroy Your perfect creation?

Jack appreciated God's explanation of how this life got to be the way it is, and he wanted to see more of what God summarized from Genesis. He had a short prayer time, updated his journal with notes of the most recent dream, and then turned to the Bible.

He read the first three chapters in Genesis, and it was captivating. Although the previous dream provided a summary, this reading allowed him to relate to the situation. He learned the first two people, who began living in a perfect relationship with God, chose to eat from the forbidden tree. They wanted to know what God knows and be like Him. Jack saw that as something good to do, but they must have had another motive. Jack reasoned they were challenging the sovereignty of God rather than merely wishing to draw closer to Him. Making the situation even more questionable was that Satan made his appearance as a friend rather than foe. That 'friend' then used lies and deception to help Adam and Eve justify their choice to eat from the forbidden tree. However, they knew what they were doing and convinced themselves they had an excuse if confronted by God. Of course, God responded with the promised consequence, and their explanation was not considered.

That reminded Jack of his my-way approach because he had allowed Satan to deceive him with a popular song and a college experience of scaling grades. He was learning that his excuse and plea would not be considered when Jesus dismisses many professed Christians.

Another observation was God's 'very good' creation immediately began to destruct as He said it would. Jack noted God did not attempt to stop what was happening. He did not interrupt Adam and Eve before they ate from the Tree of the Knowledge of Good and Evil. And then before destruction and death began, God did nothing to keep it from happening. It was like He knew the outcome when He created the test for man with the forbidden tree. Jack hoped God would explain why He allowed all of that to happen and why He allowed Satan to encourage man's separation from Him.

The Dream

> It was like a continuation of the previous dream as God explained the origination of sin during the creation period. "Lucifer (later renamed Satan) and his legions of angels chose to challenge the sovereignty of God. They were then cast down to earth where they convinced people to do the same." There was a pause as Jack processed that new information. He learned God did not create Satan as the enemy, but instead, Satan chose to become God's enemy.
>
> "The fall of Satan from Heaven is described in Ezekiel 28:14-17 and other verses in the Bible. *You were anointed as a guardian cherub, for so I ordained you. You were on the holy mount of God; you walked among the fiery stones. You were blameless in your ways from the day you were created till wickedness was found in you. Through your widespread trade, you were filled with violence, and you sinned. So, I drove you in disgrace from the mount of God, and I expelled you, guardian cherub, from among the fiery*

stones. Your heart became proud on account of your beauty, and you corrupted your wisdom because of your splendor. So I threw you to the earth. Although he did not become God in Heaven, Satan then made it his goal to be the god of the earth. Jesus describes him as the *prince of this world* in John 16:11.

"Satan's first recruits were Adam and Eve, as described in Genesis 3:4-5. They heard the lies and deceptions of Satan and chose to disregard God's absolute command. As such, sin and the consequences of it quickly consumed this earthly life. That is why life today is characterized by chaos, hurt, hardship, crime, and evil."

Although this was new to Jack and he saw the big picture of how Satan became part of this life, he still didn't know why God would allow that to happen. Why would He allow His magnificent creation, including people, to be destroyed?

God said Jack would better understand God's plan and purpose for life after he became a new creation in Christ. "Your understanding begins when you receive the Holy Spirit who reveals the truth of God's Word in the Bible." Knowing Jack was most interested, God went on to say His plan and purpose for this earthly life is to allow people to choose to give glory to Him and live according to His purpose. He said that preservation of this creation was never His purpose, as stated in Isaiah 46:9-10 NLT. *For I am God! I am God, and there is none like Me. Only I can tell you the future before it even happens. Everything I plan will come to pass, for I do whatever I wish.* God said this earthly life is the place for every person to choose between the

> attractions of Satan and the truth of God. Then, for those who believe and receive Jesus as Savior and Lord, this earthly life becomes the beginning of eternal life as a child of God.
>
> The dream concluded with God asking Jack to consider why he makes assumptions, rather than base his life on God's truth.

As he drank his first coffee, Jack was in awe to learn that God's plan for this earthly life is nothing like he thought. The history of Satan as the enemy, the first sin by angels, the fact that God provides a test for people to choose God, and the dominant role of Satan in this earthly life were things he did not know. These truths were helping him to see why this life is the way it is.

Then he smiled to himself as he remembered God presented him with a question for the next dream. His life was already changing.

Reflect and Discuss

Refer to the Bible verses (Ezekiel 28:14-18 and Isaiah 14:12-15) that describe the fall of Satan and the origination of sin. Then refer back to Genesis 3 to see God's clear command for Adam and Eve to not eat from the Tree of the Knowledge of Good and Evil, with the consequence of death if they did. Next, see the lies and deception that encouraged Adam and Eve to eat from the forbidden tree. Notice the excuse they presented to God along with His response. Discuss how all of this is part of God's plan for man to choose his eternal destiny.

NIGHT 12

How can I possibly avoid making assumptions in this fast-paced world?

Even before the last dream, Jack knew his life-long assumption of God grading on the curve was wrong. So, he wondered why God asked him to dig deeper into the topic of assumptions. But hey, it was God making the assignment. So, he started thinking about assumptions and again realized he had not first turned to God in prayer. He wondered if a prayer time was necessary because his nights were filled with God-dreams, and now he was working on a topic God suggested. It was tempting to get on with it, but that would be back to his my-way approach. So, Jack began with a prayer that God would guide him in his thinking about assumptions. He also thanked God for blessing him with these dreams.

He went to the board and listed situations when he assumed something because he was unsure of the truth. Some were simple, like dressing for the day without checking to see the weather. Another example was preparing a consulting proposal based on assumptions of what the client expects regarding change and cost. And then there were assumptions about what his wife might be thinking about their relationship, family activities, etc.

It seemed like everything he did was based on one assumption or another. Assumptions could not be avoided, and the results were sometimes good. In situations when there is a time urgency, he had to act immediately based on what he assumed to be true. But then he got honest with himself and admitted there were times when he created assumptions to justify doing something for immediate satisfaction, pleasure, control, or rage. He also thought about a business process used to manage assumptions. The Project Management function includes a methodology to minimize the risk and impact of assumptions. While there was a cost of doing that, the result was always better than not acknowledging them.

Jack concluded assumptions are part of life. However, with some effort to know the truth, the risk and damage of assumptions could be minimized. At the same time, doing that in this fast-paced world seemed impractical.

The Dream

> The dream began with God saying it was good to start every day in prayer. "There is no commandment requiring prayer first, but it is a practice that works to draw on the grace and divine resources of God for your day. The apostle Paul took prayer to the next level as he wrote in 1 Thessalonians 5:17: *pray continually*." Knowing that would raise more questions, God said it could be discussed in a future dream, or Jack could go to the Bible and see prayer examples in the lives of Jesus and Paul.
>
> Regarding assumptions, God praised him for admitting he occasionally creates false assumptions to justify something for his satisfaction. Another of Jack's findings was that assumptions had to be made because it was not easy to know the truth. "That is where a relationship with God comes in to play. With a mature relationship, a believer has an

ongoing communication link with Jesus through the Holy Spirit. He knows the truth of God's Word from the Bible rather than having to make erroneous assumptions that are often based on lies and deceptions of the enemy."

God said that both the Old and New Testaments provide the background and specifics of truth that people need for situations they face every day. As believers grow to know God and His Word through the Holy Spirit, they become empowered with knowledge and wisdom to understand how to handle each situation according to God's will. By knowing the truth, they avoid assumptions that result in harm to themselves and others.

Because Jack was thinking about the topic of truth, God referenced Jesus' answer to Pontius Pilate when He was on trial for His life. "As a Roman who did not want to be in the middle of a Jewish conflict calling for the death of Jesus, Pilate asked Jesus to help him with a defense. As shown in John 18:37, Jesus answered, *'In fact, the reason I was born and came into the world is to testify to the truth.'* Pilate's sarcastic reply was, '*what is truth?'* Most people do not think that truth is absolute. They assume truth is relative, but it is not.

"Although a believer is not always able to recall a specific verse, your knowledge of the Bible's message, together with the Holy Spirit's counsel, provide what you need for your thoughts, words, and actions to be based on God's truth."

What a dream! Jack learned truth exists and is readily available. He had become much like Pilate, who sarcastically said, "What is truth?" He thought about news stories, television shows, and movies where truth is twisted into lies and deception. He recalled an old TV series called Spin City that glorified the art of spinning truth. The show is long gone, but the practice is the norm.

Jack thought back to what happened when Satan first introduced lies and deceptions that were accepted as truth. Before long, people could not distinguish the difference. Although he admitted God's truth is readily available, it still seemed like a monumental effort to understand the Bible enough to avoid making erroneous assumptions. Plus, he was still concerned about how his life would change when he committed to going all-in with God's truth.

Reflect and Discuss

Think about the assumptions you make. You may find some are based on truth, while others are not. Some have minor consequences, while others can change lives. Do you believe knowing the Bible's overall message and specific verses can help in the words you say and the actions you take?

Identify some situations where your assumptions had good and bad results. Think about assumptions that resulted in financial gains or losses and those that affected your relationship with family, friends, and associates.

NIGHT 13

How will my life change after I become a new creation in Christ?

Jack was beginning to accept one facet of his new life in Christ would be to study the Bible. That would provide him with wisdom from observing the interactions of God with generations of people. From his brief introduction to the Bible, he knew it contained useful lessons for his life. He also thought it was most interesting that reading the Bible could be a catalyst for personal communication with God through the Holy Spirit, somewhat like the dreams.

He saw the Bible as a critical element of his future life, but in the meantime, he wanted to know other ways his life would change. He was now interested in getting close to God but was still reserved because he loved his life. At the same time, Jack was beginning to admit his definition of a good life may be shallow.

The Dream

God said He would use one of Jesus' stories from His Sermon on the Mount to help answer Jack's question. *Enter by the narrow gate. For the gate is wide and the way is easy that leads to destruction, and those who enter by it are many. For the gate is narrow and the way is hard that leads to life, and those who find it are few.* (Matthew 7:13-14 ESV). Presently, Jack, you are on the *broad road to destruction.*

The *narrow gate* is the point of truly believing and receiving Jesus as Savior and Lord. And the *narrow road that leads to life* will be your journey forward."

To Jack's specific question, God explained that life, as he knows it today, will become very different as he travels that Narrow Road with Jesus as his Lord. Over time, Jack would have new friends, new freedoms, new values, and a new purpose. "You will think about different things and act in new ways as you follow Jesus and become the person you were created to be." He said the New Testament provides many examples of what happens as people go all-in to follow Jesus. "Paul said it this way: *My old self has been crucified with Christ. It is no longer I who live, but Christ lives in me. So I live in this earthly body by trusting in the Son of God, who loved me and gave himself for me* (Galatians 2:20 NLT)."

Knowing Jack was startled with Paul saying, *my old self has been crucified,* God explained that Paul was no longer the person he had been. He continued with that point because Paul, like Jack, had previously liked his life. "Later from experience, Paul assessed his choice to become a new person in Christ. *I am a pure-blooded citizen of Israel and a member of the tribe of Benjamin—a real Hebrew if there ever was one! I was a member of the Pharisees, who demand the strictest obedience to the Jewish law. I was so zealous that I harshly persecuted the church. And as for righteousness, I obeyed the law without fault. I once thought these things were valuable, but now I consider them worthless because of what Christ has done. Yes, everything else is worthless when compared with the infinite value of knowing Christ Jesus my Lord. For his sake I have discarded everything else, counting it all as garbage, so that I could gain Christ and become one with him. I no longer count on my own righteousness through obeying the law; rather, I become righteous through faith in Christ. For God's way of making us right with himself depends on faith. I want to know Christ and experience the mighty power that raised him from the dead. I want to suffer with him, sharing in his death, so that one way or another I will experience the resurrection from the dead! I don't mean to say that I have already achieved these things or that I have already reached perfection. But I press on to possess that perfection for which Christ Jesus first possessed me* (Philippians 3:5-12 NLT)."

God then explained the Narrow Road journey on earth is sure to include opposition. He encouraged Jack to read about Paul's life to see the hardships he endured and the resources he received from God to withstand the enemy.

"In His Sermon on the Mount, Jesus confirmed that life in Christ includes persecution. *Blessed are those who are persecuted because of righteousness, for theirs is the kingdom of heaven. Blessed are you when people insult you, persecute you and falsely say all kinds of evil against you because of me. Rejoice and be glad, because great is your reward in heaven, for in the same way they persecuted the prophets who were before you* (Matthew 5:10-12).

"However, you will have all of the divine resources you need for your life to be one of joy in Christ beyond what you know today. *But the fruit of the Spirit is love, joy, peace,*

> *forbearance, kindness, goodness, faithfulness, gentleness, and self-control* (Galatians 5:22-23)."
>
> God continued saying that all of those words describing the fruit of the Spirit will have a much deeper meaning than Jack now understands, and he will be happy with his new life in Christ. "There are many other descriptions of the joy of being a new creation in Christ, including this from Jesus' friend in 1 Peter 1:8-9. *Though you have not seen him, you love him; and even though you do not see him now, you believe in him and are filled with an inexpressible and glorious joy, for you are receiving the end result of your faith, the salvation of your souls.*"

Jack awoke with an answer well beyond what he expected. It certainly was not a sugarcoated sales pitch, but instead the truth of God's Word. He still didn't get the specifics of what would change, but he saw the big picture and appreciated the truth. He would be changed and face opposition he does not currently know. Yet, somehow, all of that results in joy, a close relationship with God, and rewards in Heaven.

The chaos and problems would continue on his Narrow Road journey, but he would have new resources from God to deal with them. He would not forget Jesus' analogy of the Broad Road, Narrow Gate, and Narrow Road as a picture of this earthly life journey. He also realized most people are on the Broad Road to destruction, and they never take the exit to live with God.

Reflect and Discuss

If you are on the Narrow Road journey, what else would you tell

Jack? If you are still on the Broad Road, what else do you want to know about life in Christ? Discuss other topics that Paul described in Philippians 3:5-12.

NIGHT 14

How fast will change take place?

He would no longer be controlling his fate but admitted he probably never did anyway. Jack just handled things on his own without the divine resources of God. He still favored his approach because it was what he knew, but it was clear the eternal consequence of his my-way approach would not be good. Going forward would require faith, but he would respectfully ask for more specifics. Hopefully, God would provide a preview of the pace at which his new life would be rolled out.

The Dream

This dream setting was the same, allowing Jack to focus all of his attention on God's message. God said Jack would start his new life as a spiritual infant, and it would take some time and effort to mature. He quoted 1 Peter 2:2-3: "*Like newborn babies crave spiritual milk, so that by it you may grow up in your salvation, now that you have tasted that the Lord is good.* As you initially taste the goodness of the Lord as a new creation in Christ, you will want to go into the world to make a difference. But like a newborn infant, you will need spiritual milk so that you can mature into the person I created you to be."

God reminded Jack although he will be on the Narrow Road to life, the billions of lost people, together with the enemy, are still nearby on the Broad Road to destruction. "Spiritual growth will be a struggle requiring your intentional effort, the truth of God's Word, the example and direction of Jesus, the counsel and power of the Holy Spirit, and the support of other true believers." He quoted Ephesians 4:14-16. "*Then we will no longer be infants, tossed back and forth by the waves, and blown here and there by every wind of teaching and by the cunning and craftiness of people in their deceitful scheming. Instead, speaking the truth in love, we will grow to become in every respect the mature body of him who is the head, that is, Christ. From him the whole body, joined and held together by every supporting ligament, grows and builds itself up in love, as each part does its work.*"

God told Jack the apostle Paul is an excellent example of going through the process of becoming mature. "Before his encounter with the Spirit of Jesus on the road to Damascus, Saul (his Hebrew name) was highly educated and regarded for his knowledge of Scripture. Upon his decision to repent and follow Jesus, Saul was not ready to go into the world to make disciples. He was an educated adult, but he was spiritually immature. Saul was forgiven but still needed freedom from the strongholds of his life. He also needed to grow to know Jesus and discover God's plan and purpose for his life ahead. He did not have the New Testament writings to find answers like you are blessed to have, but he did have a relationship with Jesus and the power of the Holy Spirit.

"Saul immediately went into prayer seclusion for three years. That allowed his relationship with Jesus to grow and mature as described in Galatians 1:11-17. *I want you to know, brothers and sisters, that the gospel I preached is not of human origin. I did not receive it from any man, nor was*

> *I taught it; rather, I received it by revelation from Jesus Christ. For you have heard of my previous way of life in Judaism, how intensely I persecuted the church of God and tried to destroy it. I was advancing in Judaism beyond many of my own age among my people and was extremely zealous for the traditions of my fathers. But when God, who set me apart from my mother's womb and called me by his grace, was pleased to reveal his Son in me so that I might preach him among the Gentiles, my immediate response was not to consult any human being. I did not go up to Jerusalem to see those who were apostles before I was, but I went into Arabia. Later I returned to Damascus.*"
>
> God concluded the dream by telling Jack his journey to mature as a new creation in Christ would not be the same as Paul's. Still, he would need the same divine resources to grow to know God, find freedom from the strongholds of his life, discover his purpose, and begin making a difference for the glory of God.

Jack felt more comfortable knowing he would have new resources from God for his new life. He had a preview of that life with New Testament examples, but going forward would ultimately come down to faith and trust Jesus would lead and protect him in his new life.

Reflect and Discuss

If you have not yet truly believed and received Jesus, does this dream make you feel more comfortable with going ahead? If you have a saving relationship with Him, is it growing? What is your next step to grow closer?

NIGHT 15

Why do You say that everything we do should be for Your glory?

Throughout the next day, Jack continued to think about how the last dream ended. It was like God gave him additional dream topics of knowing God, finding freedom, discovering purpose, and making a difference, all for God's glory. He decided to begin by asking why everything we do should be for God's glory.

The Dream

God confirmed Jack's thought that going forward with this commitment would come down to faith and trust that God would provide whatever he would need. He again spoke Proverbs 3:5-6, which would later become a go-to verse for Jack. "*Trust in the LORD with all your heart and lean not on your own understanding; in all your ways submit to him, and he will direct your paths.*" After a slight pause, the presence of God spoke several verses relating to his question:

"I am the Lord; that is my name! I will not yield my glory to another or my praise to idols (Isaiah 42:8).

"So, whether you eat or drink or whatever you do, do it all for the glory of God (1 Corinthians 10:31).

"I will harden the hearts of the Egyptians so that they will go

in after them. And I will gain glory through Pharaoh and all his army, through his chariots and his horsemen (Exodus 14:7).

"Not to us, Lord, not to us but to your name be the glory, because of your love and faithfulness (Psalm 115:1).

"Now to him who is able to do immeasurably more than all we ask or imagine, according to his power that is at work within us, to him be glory in the church and in Christ Jesus throughout all generations, for ever and ever! Amen (Ephesians 3:20-21).

"For you were bought with a price. So, glorify God in your body (1 Corinthians 6:20 ESV).

"He said in a loud voice, "Fear God and give him glory because the hour of his judgment has come. Worship him who made the heavens, the earth, the sea, and the springs of water (Revelation 14:7).

"And if that is not enough to upset unbelievers, the fact that I am a jealous God adds to their rejection of who I am. *You must worship no other gods, for the LORD, whose very name is Jealous, is a God who is jealous about his relationship with you* (Exodus 34:14 NLT)."

God explained that many people view His expectation for glory and admission of being jealous as selfish and contrary to their picture of a loving God. "But know that love for My creations is the very reason that I am jealous to have that relationship and worship. I am life as it was created to be." God went on to say the trials, tribulations, and hardships of

> this world today are there because people are not living for His glory by following His will. In closing the dream, God reminded Jack to pray for His kingdom to come, and His will to be done on earth as it is in Heaven.

The clock read 5:30, but he did not move as he relived that dream. He understood God is jealous for people to live for His glory out of love for the people He created. Only when that happens can people experience life as it was created to be.

Reflect and Discuss

Imagine God speaking directly to you as you again read each of the verses shown above. Is there any doubt God is serious about His expectation for us to live for His glory? Review your recent few days and identify ways you have intentionally given glory to God. Also, identify some things that you are doing that God sees with jealousy because of His love for you.

NIGHT 16

Knowing God: Who is God the Father?

Jack now understood and agreed with why people should live for the glory of God. His perspective at this point was that giving glory to God would be in his best interest. Later, as he matured spiritually, he would give God glory simply because He deserves all glory.

As the end of the day approached, Jack defined 'knowing God' as the topic for the upcoming dream. Since he had much to learn, he decided to ask how to know God over three nights, beginning with God the Father.

The Dream

> The dream setting this time was spectacularly different. Jack searched for a word to describe it, and 'glorious' came to mind. But his definition of that word was an understatement of what he was experiencing. It was like God was enjoying this opportunity to tell Jack about Himself as the one true God.
>
> He reminded Jack that knowing about God is not the same as knowing Him. "Only when a person becomes a new creation and adopted child of God does he have the opportunity to grow to know God as the Father, Son and Holy Spirit. That typically takes time and intentional effort.

"You have been assuming God to be someone He is not – essentially believing in a false god. Knowing the vast truth about God is not a prerequisite for becoming a new creation in Christ, but you must be willing to drop your assumptions and turn to the truth of God's Word."

As a preview of what Jack would discover, the heavenly Father spoke these verses from the Bible.

God is infinite, self-existing, and without beginning and end. *Before the mountains were born or you brought forth the whole world, from everlasting to everlasting you are God* (Psalm 90:2).

God is immutable, meaning His nature and attributes never change, providing us with assurance in all of His promises. *"I the Lord do not change..."* (Malachi 3:6).

God is self-sufficient and has no needs. *"I make known the end from the beginning, from ancient times, what is still to come. I say, 'My purpose will stand, and I will do all that I please.' From the east I summon a bird of prey; from a far-off land, a man to fulfill my purpose. What I have said, that I will bring about; what I have planned, that I will do* (Isaiah 46:10-11).

God is omnipotent or all-powerful, assuring us that His plan for life is on track and will be completed despite the opposition from the enemy. *"I know that you can do all things; no purpose of yours can be thwarted"* (Job 42:2).

God is omniscient, which means He knows everything – past, present, and future. *Great is our Lord and mighty in* *power; his understanding has no limit* (Psalm 147:5).

God is omnipresent, meaning He is always everywhere, allowing us to know we are never alone. *The eyes of the Lord are everywhere, keeping watch on the wicked and the good* (Proverbs 15:3).

God is wise with perfect wisdom. *"To God belong wisdom and power; counsel and understanding are his* (Job 12:13).

God is faithful and true, keeping His promises. *"Know therefore that the LORD your God is God; he is the faithful God, keeping his covenant of love to a thousand generations of those who love him and keep his commands"* (Deuteronomy 7:9).

God is good. *O, taste and see that the Lord is good"* (Psalm 34:8). We experience that goodness in all situations when we acknowledge Him in all we do.

God is just. *He is the Rock, his works are perfect, and all his ways are just. A faithful God who does no wrong, upright and just is he* (Deuteronomy 32:4).

God is merciful, compassionate, and kind. *All the paths of the Lord are mercy and truth, to such as keep His covenant and His testimonies* (Psalm 25:10 NKJV).

God is gracious, providing both common grace and saving grace that we neither deserve nor can earn. *The LORD is gracious and compassionate, slow to anger and rich in love* (Psalm 145:8).

God is love, well beyond our understanding of the word.

Your love, Lord, reaches to the heavens, your faithfulness to the skies. Your righteousness is like the highest mountains, your justice like the great deep (Psalm 36:5-6).

God is holy, meaning set apart and perfect in all of His attributes. *"There is no one holy like the Lord; there is no one besides you; there is no Rock like our God* (1 Samuel 2:2).

God is three persons of Father, Son, and Holy Spirit, yet He is one God. *Then God said, "Let us make mankind in our image, in our likeness…"* (Genesis 1:26). *"Therefore, go and make disciples of all nations, baptizing them in the name of the Father and of the Son and of the Holy Spirit…"* (Matthew 28:19). All persons of God have these same attributes as each is the same God.

Jack began his morning prayer time, giving thanks to God for being who He is rather than the god Jack assumed Him to be. And he knew there was so much more to discover. Rather than immediately ask the next question, Jack decided to take a few days to read the Bible to learn more about God's attributes.

Reflect and Discuss

How does this list of God's attributes compare with how most people view God? Although anyone who has attended church knows that God is love, sometimes the prevailing thought is He is more of a God of wrath and punishment. How do these attributes relate to fearing God?

NIGHT 17

Knowing God: Who is Jesus, the Son of God?

The next morning at his home office Jack went to his Bible to find more about God the Father in the Old Testament. Beginning the day in prayer crossed his mind, but one voice told him prayer wasn't necessary because he was researching the Bible and having nightly dreams with God. But another voice reminded him that, without God, nothing he does is fruitful. So, he began with prayer and then started his study on page one of the Bible. He read the same pages of Genesis after a previous dream, but this time he would be looking for God's attributes.

He immediately saw that God has unlimited power to do anything as He merely spoke the world into creation. It was also clear God acts with purpose as He created this earthly life for people to choose their eternal destination – with God or with Satan. Jack also saw God was decisive and absolute as Adam and Eve were evicted from the Garden, and death and destruction began. Although he missed it in this reading, Jack would later discover God immediately promised to provide a solution only He could provide as an indication of His love. The resolve of God was evident because He allowed his perfect creation to begin its destruction. Jack also saw God does not entertain excuses, even though Satan's deception might be excusable. He related that to his previous argument of being good enough for God to admit him to Heaven.

Jack was amazed that God revealed all of that to him in the first few pages. He would turn back to the dreams, but he looked forward to the time when he would continue his quest to know God from pages of the Bible. Jack now prayed for the Father to teach him more about the Son of God.

The Dream

The dream began, and Jack was excited, perhaps because he was more engaged with God. The most recent setting was again in place, and the presence of God praised him for his interest in knowing the truth of God's Word. God also reminded Jack he would not initially understand some of what he hears and reads because spiritual maturity takes time and effort: *Who is wise? Let them realize these things. Who is discerning? Let them understand. The ways of the LORD are right; the righteous walk in them, but the rebellious stumble in them* (Hosea 14:9). And finally, before addressing his request regarding the Son of God, Jack was reminded God is one in being and three in persons. As such, knowing the Son is knowing the Father and the Holy Spirit.

God began speaking about the Son by referring to Luke 13:23-27 in the Message translation. *A bystander said, "Master, will only a few be saved?" He said, "Whether few or many is none of your business. Put your mind on your life with God. The way to life – to God – is vigorous and requires your total attention. A lot of you are going to assume that you'll sit down to God's salvation banquet just because you've been hanging around the neighborhood all your lives. Well, one day you're going to be banging on the door, wanting to get in, but you'll find the door locked and the Master saying, 'Sorry, you're not on my guest list.' "You'll protest, 'But we've known you all our lives!' only to be interrupted with his abrupt, 'Your kind of knowing can hardly be called knowing. You don't know the first thing about me.'"*

God acknowledged Jack has always believed Jesus suffered and died to pay the price for sins, rose from the dead, made several appearances during the following few weeks, and then ascended back to Heaven. He also believed Jesus would return to earth to somehow sort out the good from the bad. Although he was still dreaming, Jack confirmed that was pretty much what he knew and believed about Jesus.

The presence of God continued saying there is so much more. The Son of God has always existed as one of three persons of God. He was the author of creation long before humbling Himself to come to earth as the Messiah. The Old Testament provides many prophecies of the Son coming to earth as the Messiah, and the four Gospels describe His ministry life on earth. The remaining books of the New Testament contain more truth for believers to know Jesus and grow in their relationship with Him. Several years later, Jack would see the entire Bible as relating to Jesus as Savior and Lord.

"Jesus' words and actions provide a wealth of wisdom and direction. The Bible describes His life, His identity, His relationship with the Father and Holy Spirit, His authority, and His mission. Jesus calls lost people to follow Him and identifies the cost and rewards of doing so. He tells of their new purpose in life and the power they receive to fulfill it. Jesus speaks on many specific topics, including comfort,

> peace, rest, hope, joy, love, forgiveness, prayer, faith, worry, marriage, money, temptation, humility, judgment, worship, evil, happiness, stewardship, and end times. His words are powerful, practical, and useful for living in truth."
>
> There was a pause as Jack saw the scope of all he had yet to learn about Jesus. But then the presence of God said, "Knowing these facts about Jesus matters not until you become a new creation in Christ." As the dream concluded, Jack was encouraged to read the Gospel of John and discover why Jesus is the way, the truth, and the life.

Jack was overwhelmed, convicted, and sad for going that far in life without even trying to know Jesus as the Son of God, Savior, and example of how to live. He had no idea what Jesus had to say about all of those topics the Father listed during the dream, but Jack was determined to find out. He briefly wondered what his life would have been like if he had received Jesus much earlier, but he now saw a new life in Christ is all about going forward rather than back. He was disappointed in himself but most hopeful in the Son of God.

Reflect and Discuss

Go back to the dream and see the many topics of Jesus' words and actions in the Gospels. Imagine being able to recall a verse and context of each as background for dealing with life and avoiding erroneous assumptions.

NIGHT 18

Knowing God: Who is the Holy Spirit?

The next two days were devoted to reading the Gospel of John to learn more about Jesus. Jack liked the fast start of that Gospel as Jesus was called t*he Word*, and it was clear He is God who always existed and always will. *In the beginning, the Word already existed. The Word was with God, and the Word was God. He existed in the beginning with God. God created everything through him, and nothing was created except through him. The Word gave life to everything that was created, and his life brought light to everyone. The light shines in the darkness, and the darkness can never extinguish it* (John 1:1-5 NLT).

He saw that John believed in Jesus as God and related to Him as a man. In verse 2:15, Jesus became angry with the people who made the Temple a place of business. In verse 4:6, he recorded that Jesus was tired. He enjoyed food and dining with others, and He was thirsty in verse 19:28. When His friend Lazarus died, Jesus was sad, and He cried as stated in verse 11:35. John described examples of both the divine and human natures of Jesus.

Jack saw that Jesus faced opposition throughout His life from the time He was born. It reminded him of his concern about the opposition he would face after becoming a new creation in Christ. And finally, he noted the Gospel of John contained several references to the Holy Spirit.

As he prepared for bed, Jack acknowledged he had much more to know about the Father and the Son, and now was asking about the Holy Spirit. He knew virtually nothing about Him except that He was somehow involved in a feast called Pentecost. Jack thought this might be another exciting dream night.

The Dream

God praised Jack for opening his mind and heart to know the Holy Spirit as the one true God. "The Holy Spirit is God on earth after Jesus' ascended to Heaven. He lives in each person who has become a new creation in Christ and provides the divine power and direction they need.

"To prepare His disciples for the time after He would ascend to Heaven, Jesus introduced the Holy Spirit with these words: *If you love me, keep my commands. And I will ask the Father, and he will give you another advocate to help you and be with you forever—the Spirit of truth. The world cannot accept him, because it neither sees him nor knows him. But you know him, for he lives with you and will be in you. I will not leave you as orphans; I will come to you. Before long, the world will not see me anymore, but you will see me. Because I live, you also will live* (John 14:15-19). *But when he, the Spirit of truth, comes, he will guide you into all the truth. He will not speak on his own; he will speak only what he hears, and he will tell you what is yet to come. He will glorify me because it is from me that he will receive what he will make known to you* (John 16:13-14)."

Although Jack read those verses the day before, it was only in this dream that he began to see how the Holy Spirit is an integral part of God's plan. God then listed ways the Holy

Spirit provides each true believer with personal communion with the Father and Son.

The Holy Spirit is an advocate and friend as Jesus said in John 14:16: *And I will ask the Father, and he will give you another advocate to help you and be with you forever.*

The Holy Spirit is a teacher who reveals the truth of God as described in John 14:26: *But the Advocate, the Holy Spirit, whom the Father will send in my name, will teach you all things and will remind you of everything I have said to you.*

The Holy Spirit is a coach providing wisdom and power to testify to lost people about Jesus. *When the Advocate comes, whom I will send to you from the Father—the Spirit of truth who goes out from the Father—he will testify about me* (John 15:26). *But you will receive power when the Holy Spirit comes on you; and you will be my witnesses* (Acts 1:8).

The Holy Spirit is the light that identifies the need for righteousness. *And when he comes, he will convict the world of its sin, and of God's righteousness, and of the coming judgment. The world's sin is that it refuses to believe in me* (John 16:8-9 NLT).

The Holy Spirit is the travel guide of truth for life on the Narrow Road. *But when he, the Spirit of truth, comes, he will guide you into all the truth. He will not speak on his own; he will speak only what he hears, and he will tell you what is yet to come* (John 16:13). *Whether you turn to the right or to the left, your ears will hear a voice behind you, saying, "This is the way; walk in it"* (Isaiah 30:21).

> "In addition to living within each true believer as an advocate, teacher, coach, light, and travel guide, the Holy Spirit provides supernatural power, allowing believers to go far beyond their natural abilities to do God's will." He told Jack to read Acts Chapter 2 to see how the apostles, who were frozen with fear for their lives, were suddenly baptized with the Holy Spirit on the day of Pentecost. "Then, with His power and direction, they boldly and effectively went public and witnessed the name of Jesus as Savior and Lord. On that day, they went from being cowardly to fearless as they led thousands to believe and receive Christ."

Jack lay still in bed as the morning light filtered through the blinds. He realized the Holy Spirit is none other than God living within each person who has been reborn in Christ. What a resource for dealing with this chaotic life! He couldn't wait to get to his prayer journal to make notes on as much of the dream as he could remember. Even if he couldn't recall everything, he knew all he heard is readily available in the Bible. God wasn't telling him anything in these dreams that hasn't already been written.

Reflect and Discuss

Reflect on the verses that describe the Holy Spirit in terms of being an advocate, teacher, coach, light, and travel guide for us as we journey on the Narrow Road to life. Imagine having divine resources of God available at all times. Also, remember it is Jesus as Lord who is speaking to you through the Holy Spirit.

NIGHT 19

What do You mean about needing freedom after becoming a new creation in Christ?

Jack was still concerned about surrendering his my-way approach but knew he was getting closer to doing just that. In the meantime, he still had the two topics of 'freedom' and 'purpose' to explore.

The word 'freedom' made him think about patriotism, but he was pretty sure God did not have that in mind. He knew Jesus died so people can be free from having to pay the penalty of sin, so maybe that was what He wanted to discuss in the upcoming dream.

The Dream

The dream began with Jack seeing Jesus' words from John 8:34-36. *Jesus replied, "Very truly I tell you, everyone who sins is a slave to sin. Now a slave has no permanent place in the family, but a son belongs to it forever. So, if the Son sets you free, you will be free indeed.* The presence of God told Jack true believers of Jesus are set free from the slavery of sin and become adopted children in God's eternal family. He emphasized freedom from the slavery of sin does not begin until a person becomes a new creation in Christ.

Another verse appeared from Galatians 5:1. *It is for freedom that Christ has set us free. Stand firm, then, and do not let yourselves be burdened again by a yoke of slavery.* Jack read slowly and realized more freedom must be available after receiving freedom from the slavery of sin.

God explained although a true believer is set free from the slavery of sin, he may still be burdened with the personal experiences and strongholds of the past and present. "It is for freedom from the slavery of those experiences and strongholds that each believer needs freedom. That freedom gradually takes place as you turn to Jesus as Lord of your life." God continued saying He provides the power and resources to become free from the slavery of those strongholds. Each true believer becomes free from those strongholds by turning to Jesus, hearing the Holy Spirit, and associating with other true believers.

Knowing Jack still wanted more, God provided examples of why people need freedom. Bitterness, rejection, fear, self-ambition, revenge, guilt, hate, insults, anger, pride, impurity, sadness, unforgiveness, abuse, betrayal, humiliation, persecution, blame, defeat, loss, shame, and failure are some of the strongholds that can carry over to a person's new life in Christ. Jack identified with a few, and he knew other people whose lives were dominated by strongholds.

God explained that some strongholds originate from a person's actions or words, while many come from other people's actions and words. In either case, Satan as the enemy uses these strongholds to keep people from becoming the masterpiece God created them to be. "Paul understood that very well as he explained in his letter to the Ephesians. *For our struggle is not against flesh and blood, but against the rulers, against the authorities, against the powers of this*

> *dark world and against the spiritual forces of evil in the heavenly realms* (Ephesians 6:12).
>
> "In Matthew 11:28-30, Jesus offers this invitation. *Come to me, all you who are weary and burdened, and I will give you rest. Take my yoke upon you and learn from me, for I am gentle and humble in heart, and you will find rest for your souls. For my yoke is easy and my burden is light.*"
>
> The dream concluded as the presence of God told Jack some believers accept strongholds as God's will for their life. Instead, God provides His children with divine resources to be free and make a difference for His glory.

What a new perspective on freedom and hope for the future! As he prepared for the day, Jack felt fortunate that many of those strongholds were not part of his current life as far as he knew. At the same time, he acknowledged he was not the person God created him to be, so something must be holding him back. Freedom from all of his strongholds would not occur immediately upon becoming a new creation in Christ. Instead, he would find freedom as he turned to God's Word and followed Jesus as Lord of his life.

Reflect and Discuss

Knowing that Satan is the source of strongholds allows us to avoid blaming ourselves and others. That truth enables us to call on the divine resources of God to find freedom because the name of Jesus is more powerful than all influences of Satan.

Relate each of these strongholds to your life and identify those that might be holding you back from being the person that God created you to be: bitterness, rejection, fear, self-ambition, revenge, guilt, hate, insults, anger, pride, impurity, sadness, unforgiveness, abuse, betrayal, humiliation, persecution, blame, defeat, loss, shame, failure, and others.

NIGHT 20

How will my purpose in life change when I go all-in to receive Jesus as Savior and Lord?

His life purpose had always been himself. Now Jack was about to confirm that God has a purpose for him after becoming a new creation in Christ.

The Dream

The presence of God said that Jack's purpose and approach to life would dramatically change. "Doing your own thing and being good enough to slide into Heaven will not happen. As a new creation in Christ, you will live for God's glory by following Jesus as the Lord of your life." God continued by showing him two verses, where the apostle Paul described his purpose and commitment to it.

So, whether you eat or drink or whatever you do, do it all for the glory of God (1 Corinthians 10:31).

However, I consider my life worth nothing to me; my only aim is to finish the race and complete the task the Lord Jesus has given me – the task of testifying to the good news of God's grace. (Acts 20:24).

God acknowledged that Jack does not understand the depth of those words, but at some point, he will. He will need to experience life in Christ to appreciate Paul's testimony. There was a short pause as Jack reread those two verses and accepted what God was saying. He sensed that Paul spoke from his heart, soul, and experience when making those statements.

"The task the Lord Jesus gave to Paul, the task of testifying to the good news of Christ Jesus, is the same for you and for all people who become new creations in Christ. Your life purpose will be to give God glory by making disciples as Jesus commissioned all of his followers to do. *Then the eleven disciples went to Galilee, to the mountain where Jesus had told them to go. When they saw him, they worshiped him; but some doubted. Then Jesus came to them and said, 'All authority in heaven and on earth has been given to me. Therefore, go and make disciples of all nations, baptizing them in the name of the Father and of the Son and of the Holy Spirit, and teaching them to obey everything I have commanded you. And surely, I am with you always, to the very end of the age'* (Matthew 28:16-20). That assignment from Jesus is what people know as the Great Commission. It is great, both because of its purpose and because of the magnitude of the effort required. It is the purpose for every person who believes in the one true God."

Jack knew of the Great Commission but always thought it was the job for preachers, church pastors, and missionaries. His role was to donate to the church, allowing them to make disciples of people who attend. But God got his attention saying that making disciples is the job and responsibility of every true believer – and that goes far beyond donating money to the church or other charities.

God said that disciples, including those today, have many different talents and roles to fulfill their commission. "Your role as a disciple of Jesus will not be the same as the Apostle Paul or Billy Graham. Making disciples is a team activity requiring many supporting roles, and the Church of true believers is that team." He encouraged Jack to find a church that is aligned with the Word of God and filled with the Holy Spirit. He also said Jack's role in making disciples would change as he grew and matured in his relationship with Jesus. "Even though you are not yet ready to evangelize to lost people, that time will come. You will see opportunities to witness your new life in Christ to others. You may even write a testimony of your story.

"There are billions of lost people who do not know Jesus as the only way, truth, and life, and you will have a role in delivering that message. *But how can they call on him to save them unless they believe in him? And how can they believe in him if they have never heard about him? And how can they hear about him unless someone tells them? And how will anyone go and tell them without being sent? That is why the Scriptures say, "How beautiful are the feet of messengers who bring good news!* (Romans 10:14-15 NLT)."

Jack wasn't surprised to hear that his God-given purpose would be to make disciples. At the same time, he was relieved to learn there are many different roles in that commission, and he would be part of a team of believers with that purpose. He didn't know exactly how, but perhaps someday he could help other curious people like himself to believe and receive Jesus as the way, truth, and life.

Reflect and Discuss

Do you know your purpose is to give glory to God by leading people toward being disciples of Jesus? How has your role changed along the way, and what is it now? What might be your next step to provide glory to God as a disciple of Jesus.

NIGHT 21

I am ready – so please make me into a new creation in Christ.

The next day for Jack was a collage video of all of the dreams with God he had experienced. It was like he was in another world – a world in which he wanted to continue. God had been so patient, and Jack knew he could go on asking questions and receiving answers. But he was finally accepting he needed faith more than answers. There was no doubt his life would change, and Jack was still concerned about the uncertainty of a new life on the Narrow Road. Before these dreams, he believed in a false god instead of the one true God he was now committing to believe and receive. He learned so much and enthusiastically looked forward to knowing more as Jesus prayed in John 17:3, "*Now this is eternal life: that they know you, the only true God, and Jesus Christ, whom you have sent.*" He was ready.

His thoughts jumped back to the assumptions and beliefs he had before these dreams. Jack assumed he was good with God and would have been welcomed to Heaven if he had suddenly died. He assumed he was at least as good as most people, and that would be good enough to get him into Heaven. Instead of being welcomed into Heaven, Jack now understood why he would have been turned away by Jesus with these words: *"I never knew you. Away from me..."* Jack was appalled he had been avoiding the truth of God's Word for his entire life – the truth that was so readily available to him. Now he was surrendering to Jesus as Savior and Lord and was assured he was being welcomed into the family of God for eternity.

Given the myriad of thoughts running through his head, Jack was surprised at how quickly he settled into a restful sleep. His final thought as he drifted off was a simple verse from Psalm 46:10: *Be still and know that I am God.*

The Dream

The heavens of this dream setting displayed resounding joy as the presence of God began to speak. "Because Jesus paid the price, your only role, Jack, is to ask forgiveness for your sins and have an unqualified commitment to believe and receive Jesus as Savior and Lord. Believe also that only God could pay the wages of sin and provide the righteousness needed for you to be adopted into God's eternal family. As written: *The wages of sin is death, but the free gift of God is eternal life through Christ Jesus our Lord* (Romans 6:23 NLT). *God made him who had no sin to be sin for us so that in him, we might become the righteousness of God* (2 Corinthians 5:21)."

And Jack, just as Jesus rose out of that grave to new life, in the morning you will come out of your grave and rise to new life in Christ. As Jesus says to you, your eternal life with Me begins now as you are resurrected from death to life. *"I tell you the truth, those who listen to my message and believe in God who sent me have eternal life. They will never be condemned for their sins, but they have already passed from death into life"* (John 5:24 NLT).

The Father knew Jack would choose to believe and receive Jesus as soon as he was fully awake to receive Him. "Your new eternal life as an adopted child of God begins then."

Because Jack was thinking he did not have the opportunity to learn directly from Jesus when He lived on this earth, the Father reminded him of Jesus' discussion with His disciples. "*And I will ask the Father, and He will give you another Advocate to be with you forever. But the Advocate, the Holy Spirit, whom the Father will send in My name, will teach you all things and will remind you of everything I have told you* (John 14:16,26). *But when he, the Spirit of truth, comes, he will guide you into all the truth. He will not speak on his own; he will speak only what he hears, and he will tell you what is yet to come. He will glorify me because it is from me that he will receive what he will make known to you* (John 16:13-14).

"You see, Jack, you have the very best opportunity to grow to become the person you were created to be. You have Jesus as your Lord, the Holy Spirit as your Advocate and Counselor, the Bible as the truth of God, the Church of true believers, and the love of your heavenly Father. Satan and his multitudes of lost people will provide formidable opposition, but always know the love of God provides everything you need to withstand that opposition. So, awake to a new life and become the person you were created to be!"

Reflect and Discuss

Do you see and appreciate the simplicity of your role in becoming a new creation in Christ? How is it that a person's relationship with Jesus and the Holy Spirit's presence within is better than having access to God in nightly dreams?

DAY 1 OF HIS NEW LIFE

Jack was out of town on business when he awoke in the hotel at 5 am – fully aware of God's presence. He had simultaneous feelings of repentance and enthusiasm and he knew this was the most important moment of his life. His endless questions were replaced by faith that Jesus would lead him through whatever he would encounter in his new life. He was genuinely sorry for all of his sins, even those he didn't know he committed because of his self-focus. Jack believed Jesus suffered, died, was buried, and rose from the dead. He did that to pay for and erase the record of his sins of the past and future. Life would change because he would be a new person, and he was allowing Jesus to transform him into the masterpiece God created him to be. He wanted his life of false assumptions to be replaced by a life based on God's truth. His usual first thought of coffee never entered his mind as he rolled out of bed onto his knees with words that flowed from his heart.

> "Father God, I believe what I read in the Bible, and I'm ready to trust in the Lord with all my heart. I'm now willing to give up living my-way, asking You to make me into the person You created me to be. At this moment, I choose to believe in the one true God and receive Jesus as the only way to be forgiven and adopted into Your eternal family. I am sorry for all of my sins, even those I cannot recall. I pray to know why You put me on this planet, and I pray that I will pursue Your will for me as I go forward in this life. I want to learn to love You, trust You, and have a relationship with You. I need peace, God, and I ask You to fill my heart with Your peace. I pray for You to replace my stress, guilt, and shame with the freedom You promise when the Holy Spirit

lives in me. Fill me with Your love that I can express to others and help me to go all-in for Your glory as an adopted child of Your eternal family."

And at that moment it happened! Suddenly, he was assured he had become a new person and adopted into God's eternal family. Jack knew Jesus was near, and the Holy Spirit was present within him. It was a sense he had never experienced before, even in his dreams with the Father. He was forgiven, and his new life was beginning! At that moment, he became a new creation in Christ, and he wanted to go out and tell the world.

Jack couldn't wait to get home later that day and tell his wife everything about that morning. He started thinking about the discussion, but then stopped to begin his new life in prayer. He desperately wanted to drop his my-way approach but could see it would take some work and help from God to change his life-long habits. He thanked God for the incredible gift of salvation and asked Jesus to lead him through his new life. But then he laughed as he realized that his prayer was ending with a question, "What should I do next?

While on the flight home, he was not dreaming as he sat back with his eyes closed. The word 'baptism' suddenly came to mind, and he knew Jesus was speaking to him through the Holy Spirit.

He had not asked about baptism in his dreams, but he remembered it mentioned in the context of making disciples. Although Jack was now assured of his salvation in Christ, he was getting the message that baptism was his next step – but he did not know why. Using a Bible app on his phone, he searched several verses about baptism and found this as the answer to his question. *That's what baptism into the life of Jesus means. When we are lowered into the water, it is like the burial of Jesus; when we are raised up out of the water, it is like the resurrection of Jesus. Each of us is raised into a light-filled world by our Father so that we can see where we're going in our new grace-sovereign country* (Romans 6:3-5 MSG).

Water baptism is an opportunity to celebrate the experience of leaving his old life underwater and being raised as a new creation. He recalled another verse from one of the dreams that said, *the old life is gone; a new life has begun!* He also saw it as a way to announce his new life in Christ to the Church of true believers. He smiled to himself, appreciating the demonstration of why he would no longer need nightly dreams to know Jesus and be known by Him.

THE NONFICTION STORY

On day one of his new life in Christ, the character Jack had a pretty good idea of how to grow as an adopted child of God. Early that morning, he experienced what Ephesians 2:8-9 says: *For it is by grace you have been saved, through faith—and this is not from yourselves, it is the gift of God— not by works, so that no one can boast.* His works had nothing to do with his salvation. Still, he learned from the Bible that works are very much related to growing a relationship with Jesus and fulfilling his purpose following the moment of salvation. *As the body without the spirit is dead, so faith without deeds is dead* (James 2:26). Jack understood doing good works in Jesus' name would be a big part of his Narrow Road journey going forward.

I say that because, in real life, I did not know what to do as I began my new life in Christ. And for some time, I pretty much sat back and waited for God to make something happen. Finally, after a few years, I discovered I needed to be proactive to grow and fulfill my God-given purpose. Because of that experience, when writing *AWAKE*, I included several dream questions relating to what Jack will be doing in his new life in Christ. Hopefully, the reader will not sit back and wait for Jesus to make something happen. Following Jesus requires our effort, along with God's direction and resources.

Aside from the dreams, much of what you read about Jack is my story. I did sit on my dock one Saturday morning, praising myself and God for the good life I had. I also extended that invitation to God to let me know if there was a real need for improvement while

I was patting myself on the back. Not long after that, God did answer but not in a dream.

His initial reply came one Monday morning in a large industrial paper mill. As director of operations, I was at a client site to assess the progress of our firm's consulting engagement. Everyone knew me and continued their morning production meeting without interruption as I walked into the room a few minutes late. Sitting in the back away from others, I settled in with my coffee and saw a Bible verse written in small letters in the back corner of the blackboard as I listened to the chatter of the meeting. Even considering that mill was located in Tennessee and the Bible Belt of our country, it seemed out of place. There were no other religious things like that in the facility. At the same time, I seemed to be the only one who noticed it was there.

The verse was Proverbs 3:5-6, which I had never read or heard before. The part of that verse that grabbed my attention was, *lean not on your own understanding*. The verse went on to say my life would be better if I would trust in the Lord and not lean on my own understanding. How could I possibly get by without my control? How could I direct a consulting firm with twenty consultants and forty clients? How could I juggle the needs and demands of my family, friends, and other parts of my busy life? That was my quick reaction before turning back to the meeting that was concluding. The remainder of that day was very busy, and I had no time to think about what I experienced. But the seed of curiosity had been planted and was growing.

My background was also like Jack's in that I was raised routinely attending church on Sunday mornings. That one hour per week provided whatever I knew about God because I never read the Bible in between. I tried to be reasonably good, and I assumed that I would eventually be admitted to heaven. I loved Sinatra's *My Way* song, and pretty much took that approach without trying to hurt people along the way.

My curiosity about that Proverbs verse wouldn't go away. I couldn't explain it then, but I now see that verse as an invitation from God. Having available time on airplanes and in hotels at night, I addressed my curiosity by going to the Bible (for the first time in my life) to find some explanation. I assumed that Proverbs verse must be out of context because people couldn't possibly get by without depending on their understanding. Rather than answer my curiosity, my look into the Bible created even more questions, and my interest increased. At one point, I realized I had a folder full of notes, verses, and more questions. My curiosity about one verse had gotten out of control.

One night I had an idea for organizing what I had learned and still wanted to know. The idea was to create a fictional story of a guy named Jack, who would receive answers to his questions from God in nightly dreams. My intent was not to write a book, but merely keep track of what I was learning. For the most part, I started writing before I knew the Bible's answer to Jack's questions. I decided to avoid going to any religious denominations for answers, but instead, go with whatever the Bible was saying. I didn't worry much about the writing, grammar, or punctuation; I just kept going with my questions and God's answers from the Bible.

Keep in mind that at that point, both Jack and I both were assumed Christians and didn't know it. I thought I was destined for heaven because I believed Jesus was the Son of God who died on the cross for my sins and then rose back to heaven. I was likely as good or a little better than most people, and the loving God would take everything into account and welcome me into heaven for eternity. Then somewhere along the journey of identifying questions for the story and finding answers in the Bible, God showed me that I was wrongly assuming my salvation. My questions then turned toward discovering God's truth about eternal salvation. The result of that writing exercise was that I (and Jack) truly believed and received Jesus, and I was reborn as a new creation in Christ.

Of course, I was more than excited about that because I had gone for over five decades without knowing that a person's efforts to be good has nothing to do with their eternal salvation. I had received His gift of grace and was saved by faith. For me, the writing helped me to stay focused on God's invitation. At the same time, the story seemed reasonably good, and I thought it would be a way for other assumed Christians to know what they were missing. I did self-publish that story seventeen years ago and got some local attention. A few churches used the book and study guide for Sunday School classes and Small Group studies. Other people encouraged me, so I thought I was off to a good start with my new life.

However, I was again making assumptions about what Jesus expects from His followers. I had diligently pursued the Bible to discover my need for salvation, but I neglected to go beyond to see what God tells us to do with new life in Christ. I did not realize, but my relationship with Jesus had stalled because I was waiting for Him to do something. I had more or less stopped reading the Bible and had no idea of God's plan and purpose for my life. I was still enthusiastic and made a few attempts to lead others to know Christ, but I saw that I wasn't up to the task. I did pray more often but typically did not go to the Bible for direction. I was back to leaning on my understanding rather than turning to God. I wasn't refusing to follow Jesus; I was merely neglecting to go to the Word of God and the Holy Spirit to know His direction.

That went on for a few years until I became interested in writing *My Way Take 2* and *Assumed Christianity* as nonfiction accounts based on the same theme of erroneously assuming salvation and purpose. That writing allowed me to know how to live as a new creation in Christ. It was the spiritual milk I needed to grow from being an immature child of God.

People neither have to write books nor have a divinity degree to know Jesus and be known by Him. However, we must be intentional to follow Jesus rather than sit back and wait for Him to make something happen. He already made something happen to give us new life. Prayer, the Bible, friends in Christ, and a church that is firmly grounded in the truth of God's Word and filled with the Holy Spirit have become the foundation of my life.

This book, *AWAKE To A New Life*, is intended to give the reader a preview of what a new life in Christ can be. For people who are assuming their saving relationship with Jesus, I hope to convey that going all-in with Jesus is worth the faith commitment. He made it possible, and He is calling you to be adopted into His eternal family. For those people who are a new creation in Christ, but stalled in their relationship with Him, I hope this provides encouragement and direction to grow to know God, find freedom, discover your God-given purpose, and make a difference for His glory.

This story is my testimony of Jesus' prayer. He first prays for the disciples who have been following Him and then prays for believers who know Him because of His disciples' testimony. *"I am not praying only on their behalf, but also on behalf of those who believe in me through their testimony, that they will all be one, just as you, Father, are in me and I am in you. I pray that they will be in us, so that the world will believe that you sent me.* (John 17:20-21 NET). I pray Lord that many assumed Christians will believe and receive you through my example and testimony in these books.

We are not in heaven yet, but a new life in Christ is a taste of heaven as we pray for His kingdom to come and His will to be done, on earth as it is in heaven.

ACKNOWLEDGMENTS

At least in my case, it took a team effort to get me from being an assumed Christian, seventeen years ago, to writing this book. My gratitude and blessings extend to the guy who introduced me to the Proverbs 3:5-6 verse, to the people who encouraged me to see beyond my assumptions, to people who likely prayed for me, to Jesus who carried me through the Narrow Gate, to my family and friends who accepted and welcomed me as a new person, to the authors, pastors, and Lord, who continue to help me grow closer to God. I pray that these words will encourage someone to accept God's invitation to become a new creation in Christ. And I encourage other believers to take their next step to know God, find freedom, discover their purpose, and make a difference for God's glory. Jesus calls the plays, and the Holy Spirit provides the communication and power for His disciples to make that happen – and I am forever blessed to be part of His team.

ABOUT THE AUTHOR

Al Sikes uses the pen name, A.D. Sikes, and has been writing for seventeen years. All three of his books focus on the theme of assumed Christianity. He is stuck on that topic and continues to be amazed that, for fifty-five years, he wrongly assumed a saving relationship with Christ. He thought he was good with God, but discovered God did not see him that way. Not until his relationship with Jesus began, did he realize what he had been missing. As he says, "I didn't know what I didn't know."

With an engineering degree and graduate business studies, Al's first career was in the electric power industry, followed by a management consulting practice for the last 25 years of his professional career. He continues to be involved to a limited extent, but his focus is to help lost people know what they are missing by not having a real relationship with Christ Jesus. He is doing that and enjoying life with the support of his wife of forty-nine years, along with their two daughters, their husbands, six grandchildren, and a couple of foster grandkids.

Other Books by A.D. Sikes

- *Assumed Christianity* – This book addresses the fact that the current 2.3 billion self-proclaimed Christians have many different understandings of what it means to be a Christian. While that may not matter to some of us, it does to the one who does matter – Christ Jesus! Copyright 2019.

- *My Way Take 2* – The author's story of living My Way, like the song originally sung by Frank Sinatra. Copyright 2018.

I welcome your comments and story:

al@assumedchristianity.com

Made in the USA
Middletown, DE
10 December 2022

16632656R00066